WILD ZOO TRAIN

CARMELA LaVIGNA COYLE ILLUSTRATED BY STEVE GRAY

MUDDY BOOTS
Guilford, Connecticut

Published by Muddy Boots
An imprint of Globe Pequot
MuddyBootsBooks.com

Distributed by NATIONAL BOOK NETWORK

Copyright © 2017 Carmela LaVigna Coyle
Illustrations © 2017 Steve Gray

British Library Cataloguing-in-Publication Information available

Library of Congress Cataloguing-in-Publication Information available

ISBN 978-1-63076-306-0 (hardcover)
ISBN 978-1-63076-307-7 (e-book)

Printed in Yuanzhou, China

Express-ly for Nick and
his freight-train-hopping Grandpa Teddy.
—C. C.

To Cindy...Since we met
life has been a wonderful adventure!
—S. G.

"All aboard the Wild Zoo Train!

First stop—CANYONLANDS!" calls the conductor.

"Grab a water bottle, my friends!"

"Wait for us!"

"Hop on!"

"Hmmm, I don't see it on the zoo map."

Choo-
Choo-
Choo-

goes the
Wild Zoo Train.

Ding-ding-ding
goes the bell on the roof.

Clickety-clack
go the wheels on the track.

TOOOOT-TOOOOT
goes the whistle on top.

And the train slows . . .

CHOO

OOOOOOOOo

. . . in the canyon.

Watch for . . . lizards and hogs, coyotes and frogs;

cacti and cats, vultures and bats!

"I want to go too!"

"I've never been in a jungle before."

"Will we see monkeys?!"

Choo-choo-choo goes the Wild Zoo Train.

Ding-ding-ding goes the bell on the roof.

Clickety-clack go the wheels on the track.

TOOOOT-TOOOOT goes the whistle on top.

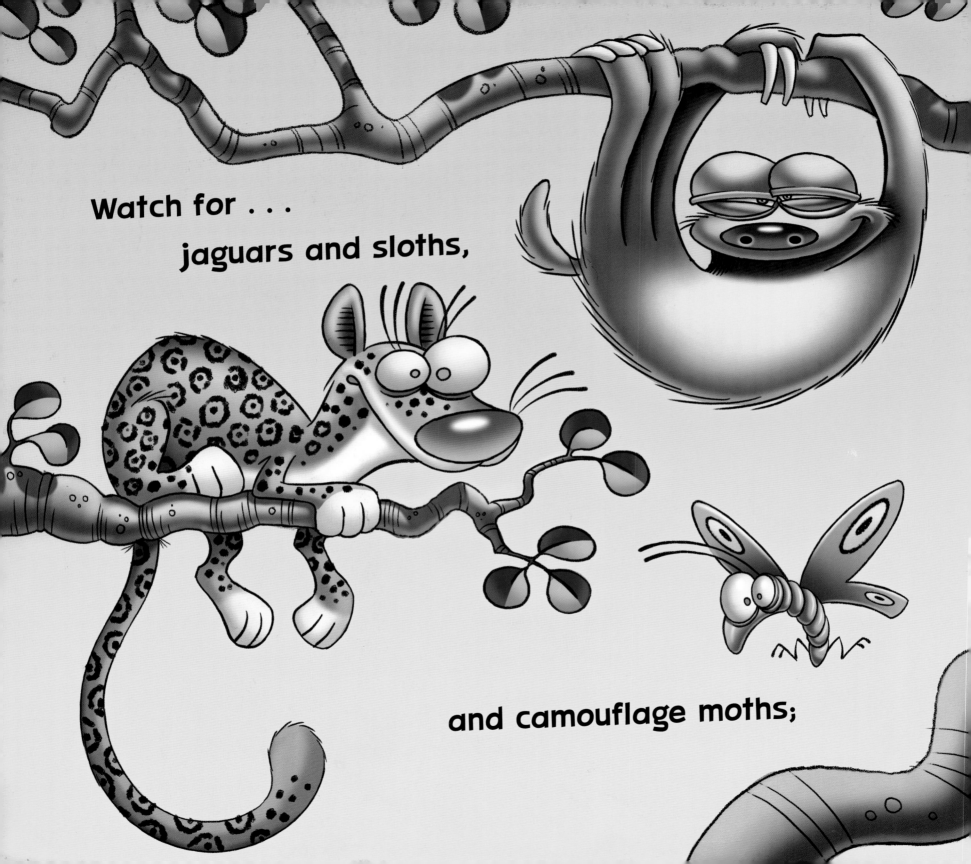

Watch for . . .

jaguars and sloths,

and camouflage moths;

toucans in trees,
and howler MONKEYS!

"All aboard!
Next stop, the AFRICAN SAVANNA!"
calls the conductor.
"Sunglasses ON!"

Choo-choo-choo goes the Wild Zoo Train.

Ding-ding-ding goes the bell on the roof.

Clickety-clack go the wheels on the track.

TOOOOT-TOOOOT goes the whistle on top.

And the train slows . . .

CHOOOOOOOOOOO

. . . on the savanna.

Watch for . . .
zebras and cheetahs,

baboons and hyenas;

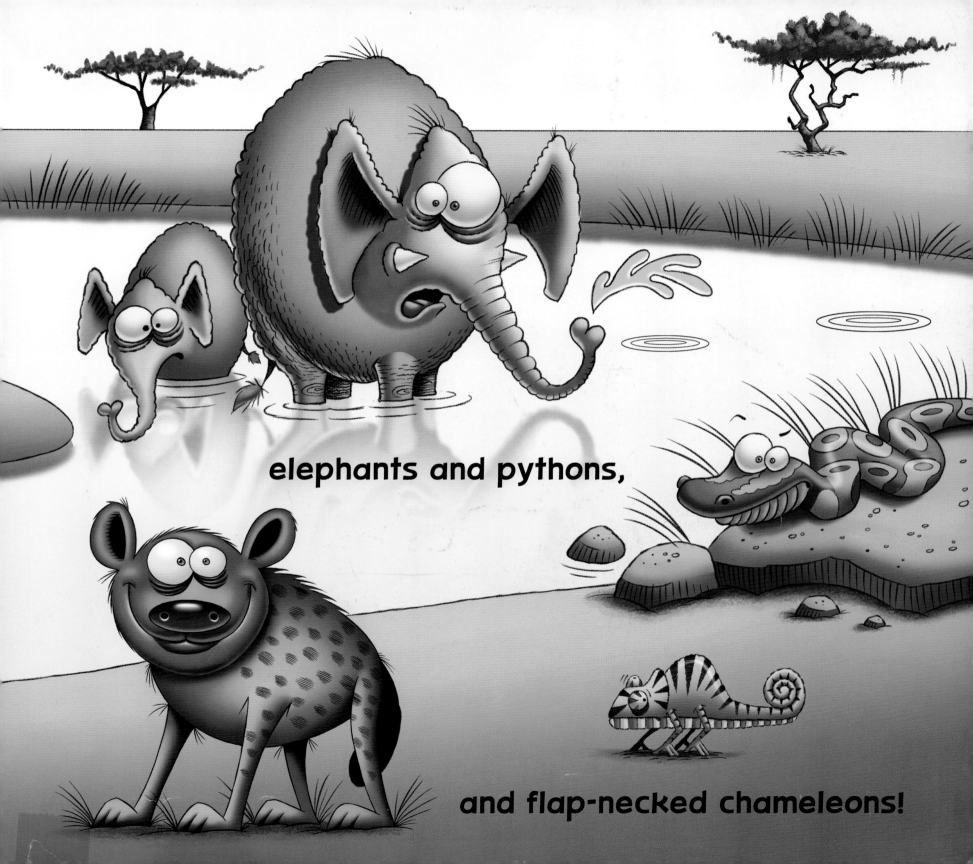

elephants and pythons,

and flap-necked chameleons!

"Next stop, ANTARCTICA!" calls the conductor.

"Parkas please!"

"Wait up!"

"Don't leave without us!"

"Isn't the Antarctic frozen?"

Choo-choo-choo goes the Wild Zoo Train.

Ding-ding-ding goes the bell on the roof.

Clickety-clack go the wheels on the track.

TOOOOT-TOOOOT goes the whistle on top.

And the train slows . . .

CHOOOOOOOOOOOo

. . . in Antarctica.

So many penguins
at this wild zoo!

Whoops, almost forgot
the long-tailed gentoo.

ABOARD!

Next stop. . .

. . . the MOON!!"

"That's definitely not on the zoo map."

"Buckle UP! TEN-NINE-EIGHT . . ."

Choo-choo-choo goes the Wild Zoo Train . . .